D0457222

I AM BAYMAX

By Billy Wrecks

Random House 🏠 New York

WITHDRAWN

I am Baymax.

I am a robot.

My best friend is
a boy named Hiro.

WITHDRAWN

We fly over the city
of San Fransokyo
and protect its citizens.

I did not always
have armor.
At first I was soft,
white, and squishy!

I was a nurse bot.

My only job was to make

people feel better.

I took care of injuries
and gave big hugs.

Hiro is a genius,
but he was not sure
what to do
with a nurse bot.

Then a masked villain attacked the city.

His name was Yokai.
Hiro knew that we
had to stop him.

When we first fought
Yokai, my soft body
got punched
full of holes.

And I deflated!

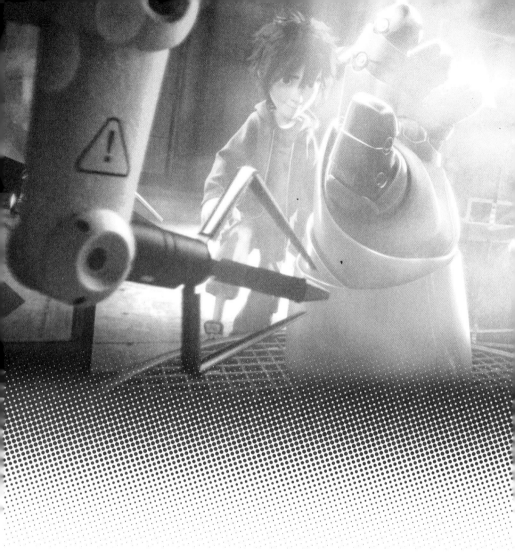

Hiro gave me
several upgrades.

I became an armored crime-fighter!

Now I can fly!

And I am super strong.

Hiro knew we would
need help to fight Yokai.
He fixed up some of
our friends, too!

With his new laser gloves,
Wasabi can cut through
anything!

Honey got a shoulder bag
filled with chemicals she
uses to fight bad guys!

Fred loves comic books
and monster movies.
Now his suit breathes fire
and super bounces!

Go Go got wheels.

Now she can move

at super speed!

We became Big Hero 6!
Together, we defeated
Yokai!

We have defended
our city ever since.

No matter what, there is
no challenge too big
for us to face.

CONTRA COSTA COUNTY LIBRARY

31901056353347